It's MY Future

Should I Be a Nurse Practitioner?

It's MY Future

Should I Be a Nurse Practitioner?

Elaine Wick

Illustrations by Michele Tremaine

The National Association of Pediatric Nurse Practitioners
Cherry Hill, New Jersey

First United States edition.
First published in 2004.

Library of Congress Cataloging-in-Publication Data

Wick, Elaine.
  It's MY Future: Should I Be a Nurse Practitioner? /
  National Association of Pediatric Nurse
  Practitioners —
      First U.S. ed.
  Summary: 11-year-old Nikki discovers her potential future career as a Nurse Practitioner through helping her brother.
      72pp
  Includes Glossary.

  ISBN 0-974969-0-3

  [I. Nursing — children's fiction.]

                                                    2004101764

Published in the United States.

Visit the publisher's web site at www.napnap.org

10 9 8 7 6 5 4 3 2 1

PRINTED IN THE UNITED STATES OF AMERICA

Illustrations by Michele Tremaine

Contents

Acknowledgments

The author gratefully acknowledges the following people for their assistance and support:

Connie Lierman, a perfect PNP/advanced practice nurse-role model, for sharing her expertise and passion for her work; and the dedicated staff of the Community of Hope Health Services in Washington, DC for their hospitality.

A big thank you to Northern Virginia writers Cathey Frei, Terry Jennings, Valerie Patterson, Barbara Roberts, Michele Tremaine, Bebe Willoughby and Della Yannuzzi for their tireless reviews and encouragement; to Andy Wick for his resourcefulness; and especially, to Lee Wick, for always believing.

Special thanks to Hanah Groeninger, Wesley Roberts and Emma M. Feeney, for giving a child's-eye view; and to Trish Groeninger for a valued teacher's perspective.

Thanks to the leadership of the National Association of Pediatric Nurse Practitioners, especially the following Pediatric Nurse Practitioner/Advanced Practice Nurse readers: Margaret Brady, Mary Margaret Gottesman and Richard Ricciardi, for providing a discerning eye and critical feedback. Kudos to Karen KellyThomas for her unwavering enthusiasm in this adventure.

*For Nurse Practitioners
and Advanced Practice Nurses
Everywhere*

Chapter 1

To the Rescue

"I see you! Do you think you're hiding back there?" I called.

When Sam didn't move, I pushed my way through the juniper bushes. I could see his suntanned legs and red T-shirt but a tree blocked his face. Usually by this time in hide-and-seek we'd both be laughing at being found.

Then I heard the wheezing sound. Sam rolled over onto his back and started to cough. He couldn't get enough air into his lungs because of the asthma. He was having an attack.

"Hurry! It's bad this time," he gasped.

I ran to the house to get Sam's inhaler. My mother was next door and there wasn't time to get her. But I knew where it was, since we always kept it in the same place.

When I got back, Sam was sitting up, still wheezing and coughing.

I handed him the inhaler. "Press down and breathe in. Then hold your breath while I count to five."

Sam pressed on the inhaler and took a big breath.

I started to count as I sat down behind him. Sam leaned back. He's only seven, so I wrapped my arms

1

around him. "You'll be okay," I said.

"Nikki? Sam? Where are you?"

"Mom! Sam's having an attack!"

My mother came running across the back yard.

"He's a little better now. He used his inhaler, but I can still hear the wheezes. Should we take him to the clinic?" I asked.

Mom listened to Sam 's breathing for just a second. "Let's go. Put your arms around my neck," she told Sam, then lifted him up and started toward the car.

"I want Winkie," Sam said.

"I'll go get him. Meet you at the car."

I ran back to the house and grabbed Sam's favorite stuffed animal, Winkie Wombat. My hands were shaking a little. I wished I could see when these attacks were coming on. I knew that Sam needed to be with somebody when he played hard outside. Maybe I shouldn't have let him hide from me.

I rode in the back seat with Sam and let him rest against me. He usually liked me to sit close when he didn't feel good. I watched him breathe hard. "It's okay if he uses the inhaler again, isn't it, Mom?"

"Yes, go ahead."

I try to help whenever Sam has a bad attack. Mom always thanks me for staying calm and helping Sam to relax. I like helping people, and now that I'm eleven, I think there must be some good ways to do more. So I've been looking around for something special to do this summer. That is, after I go to the beach with my best friend Amy.

We drove straight to our clinic with the big blue-

and-white sign saying "Community Family Clinic." Mom doesn't like to go to the emergency room if she can help it and besides, it's miles away. She carried my brother to the main desk and explained the problem. Everyone sprang into action.

"I'll call your nurse practitioner," the lady at the desk said.

Before we could even sit down, Connie Estrada was there, motioning us all to follow her to the examination room.

Chapter 2

Breathing Easier

W hat I like best about Connie is that she is so calm, no matter what's going on. And friendly. When we first met her she told us all just to call her Connie.

Mom sat in the main chair in Connie's room, holding Sam in her lap.

"Sit here beside my desk," Connie said to me. "Your mom said you found Sam having an attack."

"Yes, and he's breathing lots better now after using the inhaler," I said. "When I found him he could barely get any air in."

"That's exactly what his inhaler is supposed to do. It's good you saw the problem and acted fast. You'd make a great nurse!"

"Thanks. My dad says that, too."

Connie sat down on a swivel stool across from Mom and Sam. She watched Sam breathe for a minute.

"How did your breathing feel back in the yard?"

Sam pointed to his chest. "Like someone was squeezing me hard. I couldn't get the air in."

"Let's see what's going on. I'm going to listen to your breathing."

Connie lifted Sam's shirt and placed the round metal end of her stethoscope on his chest. Its gray tubing led to two rubber ends that went into her ears. She moved the stethoscope across his chest and his back.

"What's this cute-looking animal?" she asked when she'd finished. She patted the brown stuffed animal in Sam's lap.

"It's a wombat. They live in Australia, and they do somersaults when they play." He held the wombat up for her to get a closer look.

Sam was talking pretty well right now, and I could see that Connie was watching him breathe while she checked out Winkie Wombat.

"I want to get a peak flow reading, Sam. Remember how you did that at home to find a baseline? You know, your best breathing-out number?"

I remembered that every day for two weeks Sam blew into a tube to measure how well the air was coming out of his lungs. Mom and I wrote the numbers on a special chart to bring back to the clinic.

Connie left the room for a few minutes and came back with a peak flow meter. The tube looked like a giant thermometer with a mouthpiece attached. Sam stood up when Connie handed it to him, like he knew just what to do.

"Blow hard and let me check the number. You blow three times then I'll pick your best breathing number," she explained.

Sam started to blow. He'd been trying hard to do what Connie said since his asthma started.

Connie checked the number three times.

"Your best number today isn't what it should be. So I'm going to give you a nebulizer treatment and then check it again. Do you remember using the nebulizer?"

"You mean breathing from that mask with the noisy machine? I felt better after I did that." Sam swung his arms and gave Mom a little grin.

"That's the one." Connie turned to my mother. "I'll go have the nurse set up the nebulizer. The treatment should take about ten minutes."

"Mom, do you think I'd be good at nursing?" I asked after Connie left.

"I do, if that's what you want. I agree with your dad that you have what it takes. You really like to help people. And nursing seems like an interesting profession."

"Maybe Connie could help me figure it out. I'd ask her what she does and how she likes her job."

"I'll bet she'd like to be asked. It's a good idea to find out as much as you can about a career."

"What's hard to figure out is the difference between being a nurse and a nurse practitioner."

As I said it, Connie came back and asked my mother to bring Sam to the treatment room.

You can wait here, Nikki, or go with them, whichever you'd like."

I decided to stay behind. The examination room was cheery, with yellow walls and circus animals on a border near the ceiling. On the desk were pads and leaflets of information, like *Following Shots: How to make your child*

8

comfortable. I didn't see any medicines or syringes and wondered where those were kept. Then I remembered that the nurse gave the shots in a different room.

Twenty minutes went by and I began to wonder, so I looked down the hall.

Connie was just coming out of the treatment room.

"We gave Sam a second nebulizer treatment and he's almost finished. We'll be there soon," she said.

* * *

Sam looked like he felt a lot better when he returned. Connie sat across from my mother with the folder they called a chart. I knew there was one for everybody who came to the clinic, and Sam's chart probably had everything she'd ever written about him. She started asking my mother questions.

"Has Sam been coughing more frequently? Have you noticed when he seems to have the most trouble, like after exercise? How often does he need to use the inhaler?"

She must have asked a dozen questions and she wrote notes on the paper as my mother answered. Connie didn't seem too alarmed. Maybe that was a good sign for Sam, even though he'd sounded terrible when I found him.

She pulled out a paper that said "Sam's Plan" at the top. It was just like the one on our bulletin board at home. "I'm going to add new instructions to this and change some of his medicines," she said.

Mom asked a lot of questions and I was glad. It seemed like you could never know too much about this problem. Connie called Sam's asthma "moderate persistent asthma." She said this level was when there were signs of asthma everyday and more often than one night a week. He should continue to use his emergency inhaler as he needed it, like today.

"Now let's check a few more things, Sam. You can sit over here." Connie helped Sam onto the examination table. Mom reached over and put her hand on my shoulder. "You knew just what to do today. I'm really proud of you."

I smiled. "Before we go, I think I'll ask Connie if she'd talk with me about nursing. Sometime when she's not too busy."

"I can drive you here most any day that's good for her."

Connie finished checking Sam and helped him down. "Why don't you look in the toy box while I explain some things to your mother and Nikki."

First, Connie went over the new things she had written on Sam's Plan. As she talked I heard a strange sound coming out of the board Sam was holding. It was a wooden puzzle with a picture of a drummer in place.

"Watch this," he said and put in another piece of the puzzle. A tinny-sounding horn started to play along with the drummer and made a terrible racket.

"That's my favorite musical puzzle," Connie said. "Special exam room music." She put her arm around Sam and pulled him closer.

"Do you remember what to do when it gets hard to breathe?"

"I know I'm supposed to tell somebody right away. But I was having fun and forgot to this morning."

"Let's go over the warning signs of an asthma episode." Connie was talking to all three of us. "The signs are a little different for each person. Sam seems to be bothered by a lot of exercise and the pollens in your yard."

Sam put the puzzle down and listened. "I won't go hide when I don't feel so good."

"Whenever you cough a lot, or your chest starts to hurt, or you start breathing fast, those are all signs that you may need to use your inhaler, Sam. Also, when you get very tired or get easily out of breath."

Connie looked at Mom and me. "Since Sam's asthma seems to be triggered by exercise, he should use the emergency inhaler about twenty minutes before hard activities. I've added that to his plan."

"What activities are you doing this summer?" she asked Sam.

"Swimming. Mom says it's good for me. Nikki goes, too."

"Swimming is good. Each time you go, tell your mom afterward how it felt."

I decided I would get a special notebook, too, and write notes about Sam's breathing right after swimming.

When Connie finished and we got up to leave, I stayed back to walk out with her.

"Would you have time to talk with me someday about what you do?" I motioned back to her exam room to show what I meant.

"You mean, what a nurse practitioner does?"

"Yes. I'm trying to see what nurses do, and what I might be good at."

"Let me think a minute about my schedule."

We walked down the hall to the waiting room. Connie stopped at the desk to look at the book of appointments.

"Here's what we could do. There is so much to tell you I'd want to meet more than once."

"Oh, sure, I can do that."

"How about Wednesday afternoon at 2:00? I don't have appointments then and we can meet here and talk, if your mother agrees."

"I'll ask her, but I know it will be okay."

"You might also be interested in a babysitter's and first aid class that's being offered by the hospital education department. You can call and ask when it's held."

"Thanks," I said. "That sounds great. See you Wednesday!" I hurried to catch up with Mom and Sam.

"Mom, guess what?" I said as I climbed into the back seat of the car beside Sam.

"Hey!" I jerked my hand up off the seat. Sam's sticky toy worms and insects came with it. "What are these doing here?"

Sam sat scrunched by the window, looking the other way, giggling. There was nothing wrong with his breathing now.

Chapter 3

Emergencies Everywhere

Wednesday morning I decided to ride my bike to the library to return my books. We live on a hilly street with tall oak trees shading everything and houses with big front lawns where kids play. I started up the first hill, pumping hard, but it was too tough for me. So I got off my bike and started to walk it to the top of the hill. The ride down on the other side would be fun and the library was just around the corner.

I waved at a neighbor boy who was kicking a soccer ball around his yard. He waved back. Then he smacked the ball hard, right into the street and ran after it.

I heard the car coming up the other side of the hill before I saw it.

"Stop, David!"

David looked up and saw the car coming over the hill, but he seemed to freeze. I dropped my bike and without even thinking, I raced toward him.

"Get out of the street!" I grabbed David's arm and pulled him to the curb.

The brakes of the car screeched as it came to a stop. The driver rolled down his window. "Are you okay?"

"Yes," David said.

But I wasn't sure that we were.

The man drove off, not even bothering to get out and check on us. David started to cry. "I should've looked first."

He was my brother's friend, so I felt okay putting my arm around his shoulders. I knew he was only crying because it had scared him so much.

"C'mon. Let's go find your mom or dad."

Just then, his father came running toward us from his house. "Are you guys all right? I heard the car brakes and saw what happened."

"We're okay. We made it out of the street in time," I said. "But David's ball rolled way down there." I pointed down the hill where the ball had stopped in front of a parked car.

"Thank you *so* much, Nikki."

David's father sat down on the curb beside us. "Come on, buddy. Let's walk down and get your ball. Nikki, come with us?"

"I'm kind of in a hurry, on my way to the library," I said and waved goodbye. I got my bike and at the top of the hill I tried to get on it, but my knees were too wobbly. So I walked the rest of the way to the library, in my mind still seeing David in the middle of the street.

My dad was working on his computer when I got home. I curled up on the sofa in his office and told him what happened.

"That was really courageous, Nikki. I'm just glad neither of you got hurt."

"I surprised myself. I didn't plan it, my legs just

started running."

Dad sat down beside me and gave me a hug. "That's called the 'fight or flight' response. Our bodies react automatically to danger, and we either stay and fight or we run away."

"I guess my reaction was the right one for an emergency."

Dad squeezed my shoulder. "You're good under pressure, Nikki. What a great quality to have."

*   *   *

That afternoon, I got to the clinic right on time. Connie came out to get me and took me into a room with a big table in the middle. Pictures of mothers and children on the walls made it cheery, even though there were papers and empty coffee cups all over the table.

"We had a meeting in here a little while ago." Connie pulled the papers together in a neat pile. I collected the cups and put them in the trashcan. One folder still sat in the middle of the table with "Nikki" written across the front in big red letters.

"That's for you. I put together some information to start us off." She pushed the folder toward me.

I pulled my notebook and pencil out of my tote bag and tried not to look nervous. I've always been a little shy, and even though my teachers say I'm very good with words, I don't think I could be a reporter or lawyer, but maybe a librarian. It was a good thing I'd written down my questions before I came.

16

"I'll bet you have lots of questions for me," Connie said, as she sat down beside me.

I decided to jump right in. "I have a few. Like how did you decide to be a nurse practitioner?"

"Well, that question has a long answer. First, tell me, how are you today?"

"I had kind of a bad morning," I said, my eyes getting a little watery. I explained what had happened with David and the car.

"You look really calm to have been through all of that." Connie smiled like she understood.

I tried to smile back. "How do *you* stay so calm? Your clinic always seems so busy."

"Sometimes it isn't easy. But I keep going even when it's hard. One thing for sure is that I learn something from every tough situation. So I try to think, how could I do this better the next time?"

"I wondered that after I found Sam," I said. "Whether I could have done something else to prevent his attack."

"Maybe yes, maybe no. You did just the right thing by getting his inhaler. The main thing is, do you think you know enough about his asthma to help him the next time?"

"Yes. I read Sam's Plan when we got home and talked it over with Mom and Dad. We even tried out some 'what ifs' to see if we all knew what to do. Sam, too."

"Good. Would you like a glass of juice? I'm going to get one for myself."

I said sure, and looked around the room at the pictures of mothers and children while she was gone.

"Do you like those?" Connie asked, returning with two glasses of what looked like cranberry juice. "They're by an artist named Mary Cassatt."

I walked over to a picture and looked more closely. Small print at the bottom said *Children on the Shore*. The children playing in the sand looked so real.

I moved to the second picture.

"*Portrait of a Little Girl*," I read. "I know just how this girl feels, all tired and bored in that big chair."

"And see how the girl is in a world all of her own?" Connie said. "The artist painted her gaze to the side so she isn't looking at us."

I could tell Connie knew a lot about this art. Just like she knew a lot about children.

"I think it takes something special to be able to paint pictures of mothers and children like this," Connie said as we returned to the table.

"The artist must have loved kids a lot." I tried to think of some intelligent things to say about the pictures. For sure, I was going to ask Mom to take me to the art gallery this summer.

"They say she did. And that's the kind of caring about people it takes to go into nursing. You want to *see* how people are feeling. Some people paint what they see and some of us do work like nursing."

"That's what compassion is, right? When you really care about people and respect them." I had looked up that word last school year for a report.

"Is that why you might like nursing?"

"I think so. I know I don't have to decide now. I'd just like to know what kind of person I'd have to be. Smart like you, for sure."

"That's what is so good about this profession! Nurses are really smart along with being compassionate. You should also have integrity. It means being someone that people know they can trust to keep their promises."

I took a big drink of my juice and thought about that. I usually kept my promises.

Connie pointed at the folder that said Nikki. "This is for you to keep, so you can write in it while we talk, if you want."

I turned to the first page. There were typed sentences with spaces in between, probably for my notes. She was really organized.

"Take a minute and read that." Connie pointed to a paragraph that said *Advanced Practice Nursing.*

I read the words slowly, trying to understand what they meant. It talked about nurses getting a master's degree and special requirements.

"I know about master's degrees — my dad has one."

"Great. I have a master's degree as a pediatric nurse practitioner, so I'm called an advanced practice nurse. But I'll tell you more about that later. Let's talk about basic *nursing,* because that's what you have to study first."

I pulled the folder closer so I could start writing.

"Where it says bachelor's degree, that's the information about basic nursing school."

I started to read out loud, but I didn't get very far with

the new words — *anatomy, pathophysiology* and *pharmacology.*

"What do these words mean?"

"*Anatomy* is the study of our body. *Pharmacology* is learning about medicines and their effects. *Pathophysiology* is understanding how the normal body changes when a person gets sick or her health changes."

I jotted things down under the headings in my folder as she explained each subject on the list.

"When do you get to take care of sick people?" I asked, sliding my finger down to a line that said *Applications.*

"Right there — application of what you've learned. You spend time in different places like hospitals or nursing homes or birthing centers or clinics. A teacher is with you to supervise. We call it *clinical practice.*"

"I guess you also find out what you don't know. But I see some subjects I might be good at, like anatomy and nutrition."

"I think you'd be good at lots of subjects. You seem very smart to me."

I smiled, feeling a little embarrassed. "When you finish school, then you just go to work?" I asked.

"Yes. In your first job, nurses with experience help you get started."

"Was your first job like the nurse at the clinic who gives shots?"

"Not exactly. Like her, I was a registered nurse starting out in my career. But my first job was at a hospital working with children."

"With little kids or big kids?"

"All ages. With children who needed surgery. You know, operations."

"Wasn't that hard?"

"A little, but I liked it," Connie said. "There was a lot of teaching for both the children and the parents. I could tell you a story about a little boy I took care of."

"Okay." I sat back and accidentally knocked my tote bag onto the floor. Sam's toy stethoscope popped right out of the bag.

I jammed it back down into the tote. That Sam!

"This must be one of my brother's jokes. He's always jealous of things I do."

"Like what?" Connie asked.

"Like, he's mad that he can't do the butterfly in swimming and that I'm getting so good. I might even go out for the swim team next summer."

"What's Sam good at?"

"Dad pitches a baseball to him and says Sam's a natural. Me, I can't even hit the stupid ball."

"So you each sparkle in your own way. That's good. You don't have to compete with each other. Maybe we should think of a way Sam can be a part of what we're doing here."

"I guess so," I said. Connie was right. Sam had really wanted to come with me today.

"Let me tell you that story about my first job. It's about Josh-who-hated-needles," Connie said.

"Here's the story. When I first started working in the hospital, I think I hated seeing children get stuck with needles as much as they hated getting them."

"One day, I came into Josh's room and he was hiding under the covers. Josh was only five years old, and he needed to have a bone operation."

"When I asked him to come out and talk to me, he screamed, 'No! You can't make me.' He said he knew I was there to give him a shot with a needle."

I interrupted Connie and asked, "Weren't his mother and father there?"

"No, but they were on their way. So while I tried to coax Josh out, with him still screaming, the call came from the operating room to tell me to bring Josh."

"What did you do?" I asked, feeling sorrier and sorrier for Josh.

"This was becoming a real problem. First of all, the operating room had a schedule to keep. Then his dad walked in and Josh cried all the harder because he wanted his mother, too."

"So what happened?"

Connie started to answer but just then, a man rushed into our conference room. "Connie, we have a situation and I need you." His voice sounded worried.

"Be right there. Nikki, this is Dr. Trent. Why don't you look over the folder and I'll come back and let you know if we can keep going."

"Okay," I said, wishing I could go with her. I turned back to the folder and started to re-write my notes. Ten minutes passed quickly.

"We have to finish up for today," Connie said from the doorway. "I need to stay with this patient and his mother.

I'll call you."

"Is everything okay?"

"Let's just say it's a behavior problem that I know how to handle. But I didn't finish the Josh story, did I? Why don't you write your own ending to the scene with Josh and tell me what you'd have done. Bring it the next time we get together and I'll tell you what really happened."

"I'll try. Hope I can figure it out."

Connie thought for a second. "There's usually more than one way to get something done. Be creative. Josh was a very scared child."

"Okay," I said. At the moment, I couldn't imagine how I would get that job done.

Nikki's Folder

Advanced Practice Nursing (APN) — D escribes nurses who have gone on for more study after getting their bachelor's degree in college. They study at the master's degree level and have special clinical practice requirements. They work collaboratively with physicians and health professionals to give the best possible care to their patients

Connie is an APN and a Pediatric Nurse
    Practitioner—that's a PNP.
First, she became a nurse.
(Remember to ask her what "Collaboratively"
    means.)

Degree-Courses of Study

• **Anatomy and Physiology**
    The body and how it works. Sounds pretty interesting.

• **Chemistry**
    The study of substances.

• **Microbiology**
    The study of things we can seen under a
    microscope, like germs.

• **Pharmacology**
    Medicines, what they do, how to use them.

24

- **Pathophysiology**
  How the body changes when you are sick.

- **Nutrition and Health, Health Promotion**
  Eating well and staying well. I like this one.

- **Psychology, Sociology, Anthropology, and more**
  How we think and act and live. Cool.

- **Nursing as a Profession, The Science of Nursing and How Nursing Fits into the Health System**
  These classes tell all about what Nursing is.

- **Nursing Skills and Assessment Procedures, Communications and Interviewing**
  How to talk to people and find out about their health. How to observe people and how to examine them. (Sounds interesting. Connie says I am already good at observing.)

- **Applications of Nursing with adults, children and youth, infants and childbearing women, the elderly, in mental health, in the community**
  Go to hospitals, clinics, nursing homes, birth centers (I like this one) and practice everything you learned. Do this until you get it right. Called "clinical experience." (Sounds like fun.)

Chapter 4

Getting the Scoop

Connie and I met again on Saturday at the Union Street Eat Shop where they make the best fruit smoothies in the world. Mom and Sam dropped me off. I'd invited them to come back in a little while to join us.

We stood in line to get our treats, which I paid for, then found a booth at the back of the shop.

Connie spotted my notebook right away. "How did you make out with the ending to Josh's story?"

"It was hard to write. I really didn't want Josh to have a needle. But I thought maybe he'd need one."

"So what did you decide?"

"Would you tell me the real ending first, just to see if I am close?" I asked, thinking I didn't want to be totally wrong.

"Sure. Some of the answer you might only know if you worked there. First, I asked Josh's father to calm him, and I left the room. Next, I called the nurse in charge of the operating room and we made a plan."

"I never thought of that. What was it?"

"We agreed they'd schedule Josh later so his mother could be there, too. When his mother arrived I asked her to tell Josh that he wouldn't get a shot before the operation. He might wake up with a needle in his arm, but he wouldn't

26

feel it go in."

"I wondered how that worked."

"Then Josh's mother carried him to the playroom next to the operating room. He met Brad, a nurse anesthetist. That's a person who gives the medicine that makes you sleep during operations. Brad talked with Josh and took him into another room where Josh breathed special air to help him fall asleep. When that was done, he put the needle in Josh's arm, and Josh didn't feel a thing."

I felt like patting myself on the back. "I wasn't totally off, then. How did you know to do all of that?"

"We made a lot of decisions together there. I knew the nurses and doctors in the operating room respected children's fears and would help Josh. So what would you have done?"

I opened my notebook to my notes. I'd stayed up late last night thinking this through.

"First, like you, I decided to wait 'til Josh's mother came. Maybe she had a cell phone and I could have called to tell her to hurry. Then I was going to promise to read every page of his favorite book to him after the operation, even if it was a Harry Potter book."

Connie burst out laughing. I started to giggle. Maybe I could even use that one on Sam.

"I like that. You had the right idea. Make sure the people Josh felt safest with were all present. I'm not sure about the bribery, but if you meant it, then it would be all right."

I took a big drink of my pineapple, banana and

strawberry smoothie. Maybe I did have some of the right ideas to use.

I noticed two girls from last year's fifth grade class standing in line to get served. I waved. Both of them were going to the same middle school as me in September, and so was Amy.

" I wish you could meet my friend, Amy," I said to Connie. " We've been best friends since first grade. Our families do things together, like cookouts."

" I'll bet I'd like her. Too bad she couldn't have joined us."

" I actually did invite her to come today, but her family was going away for the weekend. Can I tell you something?"

"Sure, what is it?"

"I've got a little problem. I called about the babysitter class given by the hospital and I really want to take it. But it might come at the same time as something else."

"What's that?"

"Amy's family invited me to go to the beach with them. And I want to do both things, but it might not work. Then the second class comes when my family is on vacation, so maybe I'll miss all of the summer classes."

Before Connie could say anything, Sam was at our table.

"We're here! Mom's getting our smoothies and I'm saving this booth." He pointed to the booth behind ours.

"Hi Sam. Good to see you again," Connie said.

Mom came with two tall glasses and said hello. "Let's sit down, Sam. They've got a lot of talking to do."

"What do you think you'll do, then, about your dilemma?" Connie asked.

"I don't know yet. I guess I should talk it over with everybody."

"That sounds like a place to start. While you're thinking about it, should I tell you more about nurse practitioners?"

I nodded yes because I knew I'd have to leave pretty soon with Mom and Sam.

"You asked me how I decided to become a pediatric nurse practitioner. After I worked at the hospital a few years, I decided I wanted to be a PNP so I could help children and parents learn about good health and growing up."

"Could you just be a PNP, then?"

"No, I had to go back to school to study a lot more and get my master's degree."

"What did you study this time?" I asked, glancing at my notebook. I would probably want to take some notes again. I could almost picture how I would write this up in school if we had to tell what we did over the summer.

"Here, add these to your folder." Connie pulled several printed sheets of paper out of her purse.

"I studied pediatric primary care." She pointed at the words on the paper that said *helping children to grow up healthy, and helping them with their illnesses or problems.*

I jotted some notes under that on the paper.

Then I read the next line out loud: "*Take care of children of all ages, from newborns through young adults.* That sounds like a lot to learn."

30

"It is. I tried to break it down for you under those categories."

I concentrated on reading down the paper. Something soft brushed against my face. There was Sam leaning over the back of our booth.

"Hi Sam."

"Can I listen to you talk?"

I looked at Connie.

"Why not?"

I went back to my reading. "What does this word *assessment* mean?"

"Assessment is when I ask questions about a child's growth and his health, and about the family."

"Do you mean like how he does in school? Or if he is a picky eater?" This part sounded interesting, and I remembered that Connie had asked my mother questions like this about me on our first visit to the clinic.

"That's right. I find out how the child is developing, or growing, and if there are problems, like with learning or with physical activities. I also find out what's going well."

"And like Sam, you ask if people understand things." I turned to wink at my brother.

"I try to get to know the whole family, like yours, where everyone is learning about asthma. Then I do a physical examination. I check the child over from head to toe. Do you remember when I did that for you?"

"I do!" Sam said.

I remembered, too, especially the fact that Connie had pulled a curtain around me for privacy.

31

"How did you learn all of this?"

"We took advanced courses," Connie said. "And we learned through lots of hands-on practice. Doctors and other practitioners were always there to help."

"After the assessment, I do this—*diagnosis.*" She pointed at my paper."Nikki, I have an idea. Can you come to the clinic again next Tuesday?"

I thought for a minute. My summer plans were still not very well organized. And Tuesday was just a few days away. I leaned over the booth and asked my mother. She said fine.

"I'm inviting you to come and spend a half-day with me. Let's call it your 'day with a nurse practitioner.' You'll also get to meet Crystal, who is a women's health nurse practitioner and Michael, the family nurse practitioner."

"Thanks!" I said. But I was a little confused. "I didn't know there were so many kinds of nurse practitioners."

"There are even more, like for elderly people or in critical care units at hospitals. Some nurse practitioners work in really small towns where there is no one else to give health care."

"But let's go back to your folder notes. I want to explain a few more things that you might see me doing on Tuesday. Then it will make more sense."

We quickly went through the rest of the list and I wrote notes. Connie asked if I had any questions.

I wondered, "do you ever go anywhere else to do your job?"

" Yes, I do. I give lectures at the college. And sometimes I travel because I'm on an important national committee. I help write the guidelines for our work, like what to do when we examine children like you and Sam or when we teach families."

"Really? How do you get to do that?" I asked.

"I was appointed by the president of my organization, and I'm proud to have been asked."

"Sounds like you like *everything* you do."

Connie smiled. "I do! Sometimes there's a lot of paperwork. Like the school and camp forms that have to be filled out every year. And some days are pretty busy. But I don't mind it, really, because the days are never the same. I like that each child and family is different and that I get to watch kids grow up. You feel like you make a little difference in their lives."

Sam was now standing at our table. "We have to go. Dad's waiting for me to play ball."

"We're almost finished," I said.

Connie leaned close before we got up. "Nikki, I think you'll work out what to do about the babysitter's course and vacation. Because you know how to solve problems."

My Notes in Connie's Folder

Pediatric Primary Care — Helping children to grow up healthy, and helping them with their illnesses and problems (along with the parents)

PNPs, doctors, and others give this care. (It's who checks me out every time I go to the clinic.)

Pediatric Nurse Practitioner (PNP) — Takes care of children of all ages, from newborns through young adults

This means I can see Connie till I finish high school!! ☺

Master's Degree Courses of Study — Advanced study in: Growth and Development, Pathophysiology, Pharmacology, Assessment (of physical, developmental, family and cultural aspects), Diagnosis and Management (of illnesses, minor trauma, chronic conditions, behavior problems.)
This means there is lots more to learn in these subjects to be a PNP.

Certification for a nurse practitioner — A nurse practitioner must pass a special test to be sure she or he has the right knowledge and skills.

Services PNPs provide:

1. Assessment —
- Listen and ask about:

> Connie checks out everything.

— Growth and development.

> Is he growing okay? She asks about the family, too.

— Problems in behavior.

> Like trouble with other kids or not doing homework.

— Nutrition.

> What does everybody in the family eat?

— Physical problems or illnesses.

> Like trouble walking or being real sick (something Mom and Dad can't handle).

— Do Physical Examination.

> She checks you out from head to toe.

2. Diagnosis –
• Decide what is normal or not normal.

> This is where she works it all out and maybe does some tests, like on blood or X-rays.

3. Plan of Care/Treatment --
• Return child to best state of health.

> Like with Sam's asthma, help him learn what to watch for.

• Support good health practices.

> Get shots and stay safe.

• Promote healthy nutrition.

> Like how to get picky eaters to eat.

• Suggest changes in behaviors that promote better health.

> Like getting more exercise or brushing your teeth.

• Treat illnesses and problems.

> She takes tests, gives medicines, gives advice (like staying home from school and in bed if sick).

- Work together with doctors, practitioners, pharmacists, social workers and others—
  Refer to specialists if needed.

> Talk and solve problems together, like for a heart problem.

- Make the plan with the family.

> So people can live with the plan (like Sam knows what he's supposed to do). Teaching is big for a PNP.

- Check to make sure the plan is working.

> Connie does this every time we come to see her. She changes the plan if it doesn't work.

Chapter 5

Nikki Sits In

When I got to the clinic on Tuesday most of the chairs were full with people of all different ages. I heard some strange languages, but the only word I understood was *gracias* when the lady at the desk talked to one woman.

Today I'd pulled my long hair back with my mom's plain blue scrunchie to look a little older. I felt nervous again, sort of like the first day of school, so I unzipped my tote bag to stay busy.

"Hi, Nikki." Connie came out and motioned for me to come.

"Glad you could be here today. I have two children you can probably sit in with. I'll explain to the parents why you are here. If they say no, I won't include you. You can wait here in my office while I call the first child."

She returned in a few minutes and told me to join her.

"Nikki, this is Mrs. Fernandez, and Mrs. Fernandez, this is Nikki. Nikki is observing what I do, to see if she'd like to become a nurse practitioner some day."

Connie washed her hands and sat down in front of Mrs. Fernandez. The little boy in her lap looked about four years old.

"Nikki may want to write a few things down that she sees me doing."

"That's a good idea. Do you speak Spanish?" Mrs. Fernandez asked me.

"No, but I wish I did."

"I might need to talk with Connie in Spanish," she said. "To make things clear."

I nodded. I'd probably want to study languages, too, if I went into nursing.

"Hi Miguel. What brings you and Mom here today?" Connie asked. "Let's see, I just saw him two months ago for his well-child visit."

I noticed she was reading his chart and flipping back to certain pages. Knowing Connie, she would have written everything down like she did for Sam and me.

"He's had a rash on his head for a few weeks now," Mrs. Fernandez said. "Since it won't clear up with the cream I've been using, I thought you should check him."

"I'll look at it under that strong light." Connie pointed to the examination area. She asked what kind of cream Mrs. Fernandez had used, and what else she had tried to clear up the rash.

Mrs. Fernandez explained things to Connie in Spanish, and Connie filled me in a little in English.

"How is Miguel getting along otherwise?"

Connie listened and asked more questions about Miguel's eating and his health.

I jotted down some of her questions in my notebook. This made sense, asking about everything, to be sure he wasn't sick somewhere else. I remembered that Connie said she always liked to check how children were developing.

"Let's move over here, Miguel, so I can look at your head."

Mrs. Fernandez lifted him up. Miguel seemed fascinated with the green and red handprints and footprints on the paper sheet covering the examination table.

"First I'm going to feel your neck."

Connie put on gloves and began to touch each side of Miguel's neck. She explained that she was checking his lymph nodes because sometimes those became enlarged with an infection on the head. She turned on the strong light and started to check Miguel's head all over.

"The raised red spots look like folliculitis. That's when the follicles that hair grows from become infected. Look with me. And feel here, this enlarged node," she said, placing Mrs. Fernandez' hand on Miguel's neck.

"I'm also going to take a test for ringworm, although I don't think that's what it is. Just to be safe." Connie left the room for a minute and returned with a small glass tube and some swabs. I watched her rub a swab across Miguel's rash and put it in the tube.

When she'd finished checking Miguel's ears and throat, she helped him down and pointed him toward the toy box.

I was trying to decide what else to write in my notebook. For sure, Connie had gone through that step called assessment. She had asked questions and gave Miguel a good check-up. Then she must have made the diagnosis, because she told Mrs. Fernandez what she thought the problem was and took the swab test.

Next, I guessed, she would make his plan. Sure enough, while Miguel searched for a good toy, Connie talked with Mrs. Fernandez about what she was going to recommend.

"I'll give you a special gel to clean the area and some antibiotic cream for the infection. I'd like to see him again in two weeks." Connie explained all this in Spanish to be sure Mrs. Fernandez understood. She repeated it for me in English.

Mrs. Fernandez asked a couple more questions in Spanish and thanked Connie.

I followed Connie when she went out to get the prescriptions ready in her office.

"Mrs. Fernandez understands well what to do," she said. "I know if this medicine doesn't work she'll be back to see me."

"Wait here again, Nikki. I should have a newborn baby and her parents next."

I looked at the clock. Where had the time gone? We were so busy, the day was flying by!

Connie came back for me ten minutes later. "These parents would like to talk with me alone while I take their history. They have some private concerns, but they feel fine about you coming in while I examine their baby."

As Connie started to leave, a man appeared at the door. He waved at me. "You must be Nikki. Hi, I'm Michael, the family nurse practitioner."

41

"Hi. Connie told me about you."

"She did? Well, I hope it was all good! You can come spend a day with me, too, if you want."

"Everybody can talk with Michael," Connie said. "He really understands people's worries."

Michael laughed. "And this is Zach, my student nurse practitioner. He's learning with me this semester. Connie, do you have a minute?"

Connie stepped back into the office and Michael and Zach followed.

"I want to check something out. I'm seeing a child whose immunizations were delayed for almost six months. This is what I plan to do to get her back on schedule," Michael explained.

I listened to them talk and tried to understand. A lot of the words I wasn't sure of, so I wrote in my notebook, they told each other their ideas. Solving problems together.

"Does he take care of kids, too?" I asked Connie when Michael was gone.

"He does. Michael's specialty is in family nursing. Some of our education is the same, but he also takes care of adults — the whole family, like his title says."

I didn't want to sound like a know-it-all but all of a sudden, I understood. "So the difference between you isn't exactly what you do, but it's who you do it for?"

"That and the fact that he knows a lot about adult health and illnesses. He also specializes in conditions of the heart. I'm going now, to see my newborn and her parents."

42

I could hardly wait to see this new baby. To stay busy, I scanned the titles of the books on Connie's bookshelf. It looked like there was something on every subject we had talked about. Magazines and CDs, too. She told me once that she listens to CDs about new changes in medicines, in the car on the way to work.

I went to the doorway to see what was going on outside the office. Down the hall there was a kid standing on a scale to be weighed, and the lady from the desk was looking for someone. The doctor I met before was talking with a woman with a stethoscope. Everyone seemed busy and nobody looked unhappy or stressed. This definitely felt like a good place to work.

"Okay, you can join me now."

I followed Connie into the examination room.

"Stand over here, Nikki," Connie said, then introduced me to Mr. and Mrs. Andrews and their baby.

Mrs. Andrews smiled at me and Mr. Andrews said hello. I thought Mrs. Andrews looked a little tired. Baby Melissa looked happy in her mother's arms, wrapped up in a yellow blanket. Her eyes didn't move from her mother's face.

Connie sat down, rubbed her stethoscope like she was warming it up and opened the baby's blanket. She lifted Melissa's tiny shirt and placed the end of the stethoscope on her chest, moving it to each side and to the back. Then she reached for her special flashlight and shined it into Melissa's eyes.

"Her eyes look good. I'd like to finish examining her over here."

She took Melissa from Mrs. Andrews and placed her on the bed, unwrapping the blanket. I thought Melissa was the most beautiful baby I'd ever seen and the smallest. Looking at her reminded me of the babysitting classes. Now I knew for sure I needed to take them.

"I'm going to examine her from head to toe," Connie said, holding her hand on the baby's tummy. Melissa's jerky little arms and legs waved like she was happy.

Connie felt Melissa's head all over. She studied the baby's face then put her hands on the back of Melissa's head and held her up. She moved her all around, from side to side and up and down.

"I'm watching her eyes move in each direction," she explained, then laid Melissa back on the bed.

When Melissa opened her mouth to yawn, Connie quickly took the small flashlight and a wooden stick to look inside, holding her finger on the baby's chin to keep it open. She rubbed her finger against the baby's cheek and I watched Melissa turn her head a little and her lips start to suck.

"That's called the rooting reflex."

Melissa was still quiet. I thought she probably wondered what was coming next. Or maybe little babies didn't think yet.

Connie took off Melissa's shirt and felt her neck, her shoulders, and her chest and moved her arms all around. She looked at the palms of her hands and her fingers. Connie's hands moved down to Melissa's tummy like she was pressing everywhere, but gently. Even though Melissa started to fuss, Connie pulled on examination gloves and moved down to check the baby's bottom. She talked as she went along, telling Mrs. and Mr. Andrews everything that she was doing.

Finally, when she spread Melissa's hips and knees out to touch the bed, Melissa really began to cry.

"I know you don't like this, little one. But I have to check you for dislocated hips."

When she turned her over on her tummy Melissa stopped crying. Connie ran her fingers along the baby's back and looked everything over. She turned Melissa onto her back and held her head in her hands, then lifted it just a little bit and let go. Melissa's arms jerked up and out, and her hands opened.

"That's a normal startle response, or Moro reflex. It usually lasts five or six months. It's a good test of the brain and the nerves and the muscles working well together."

"This is the palmar grasp reflex," she said, putting her finger in Melissa's hand.

I watched the baby curl her little fingers around Connie's finger, and when Connie tried to pull it away, Melissa wouldn't let go. Connie put a finger of her other hand in Melissa's other palm and that one tightened, too. Then she lifted a little and Melissa came straight up by her hands and hung on. I couldn't believe that a brand new baby was so strong.

"What a good baby. That's a normal reaction and it's strong."

"I'm a little worried about that rash on her face. My first baby didn't have it," Mrs. Andrews said

"You mean these little white bumps?" Connie pointed

to the baby's nose and cheek. "That's called milia. It's a normal newborn rash that not all babies have, and will disappear on its own."

"It does look a little better than last week," Mrs. Andrews said.

Connie wrapped Melissa in her blanket and handed her to her mother. "Everything looks very good. I'm going to fill in Melissa's growth chart with her weight and height measurements the nurse took when you arrived today."

She turned to me. "Nikki, each visit I'll look at the growth chart with the parents to see how well Melissa is growing. Next, I'm going to go over Mr. and Mrs. Andrew's questions and talk about where we go from here."

"Should I leave?" I asked.

"Thanks. That's probably a good idea."

Even though this was one of my favorite parts, watching Connie do what she was so good at—listening and talking things through—I knew when I should leave. I went back to her office to wait. When Connie returned, she explained the next step.

"Our certified nurse midwife is here today, and I'm going to have her talk with Mrs. Andrews about a breast-feeding concern. Crystal is an expert in that area. Let's see if she's free."

We walked to another office where a woman was writing in a chart. "Crystal, this is my observer, Nikki."

Crystal shook my hand. "I'm so glad to finally meet you! Connie told me you're interested in nursing. Maybe you'll like what I do. I get to work with women and babies all day long, and I just love it."

"I might like that." Actually, it sounded pretty cool.

"I have a mother with a new baby for you to see, Crystal," Connie said. "She's having some trouble breast-feeding her baby and is worried. I've gone over approaches with her, but I think she could use your expertise and reassurance. Can you see her now?"

"Sure. I'll come with you and bring her to my office."

When we were alone again, Connie explained more. "Crystal is such a good teacher and she'll reinforce what I told Mrs. Andrews. Certified nurse midwives work with women during pregnancy, then help mother's give birth to their baby, and help them afterward."

"There's a girl in my class whose mom had a nurse midwife when her baby was born. She said the nurse midwife explained a lot," I said.

"Then you already have some information about advanced practice nurses. That's good to hear. I have a few minutes for any other questions you have right now."
I looked at my notebook. "When does Melissa come back to see you again?"

"At two months, unless her parents have concerns before then. Did you understand everything I explained to them about Melissa's examination?"

"I think I got it all. You told them a lot while you were checking the baby over. It seemed like they knew exactly what you meant."

"This is such an important visit," Connie said. "How babies develop depends a lot on how well their parents

nurture them. So I try hard to earn the trust of the parents right away. Then we can work together for their baby. Melissa's mom and dad are so interested, I think they will be very good parents."

"Mrs. Andrews got really calm when you started explaining everything," I said.

"Mrs. Andrews' other concern was if Melissa could lie on her tummy when she's awake. Did you know babies should sleep on their backs?"

"I kind of remember that from when Sam was a baby."

Connie pointed to Melissa's chart. "I need to write up my notes about Melissa. That's a really important part of the whole visit. It won't be long before the clinic has electronic records, and I can't wait. Almost everything will be recorded on the computer. By the time you're a nurse practitioner, your clinic might be using telehealth, or treatment by television, where you can talk 'live' with professionals in other places."

That was all good news, since I was already using my computer every day.

"Nikki, let's talk again after you've had a chance to think about what you saw today. Maybe tomorrow?"

"Okay, I could do that." I was thinking I wanted to bring something for Connie anyway.

"Come at noon when I have my break. By the way, what did you decide to do about the babysitting course and vacation with your friend?"

"I'm still not exactly sure how things are going to work out. Maybe by tomorrow I'll know."

Right now, after talking with Connie and seeing her

work, nursing seemed like a perfect career for me. And she'd given me ideas of how to check out my thinking some more. Like volunteering. And babysitting, for sure.

Yesterday I'd talked things over with my parents and they said they'd support my decision about taking the course, either way. But when Amy called me last night with the exact dates of their vacation I told her my problem. The two-day course was offered right at the start of their beach trip.

"So you mean you might *not* go with me on vacation? You just *have* to come with us!"

"I really, really want to!" I'd said. "I'm going to try to work this out."

Now I didn't want to think about how it would be if I lost my best friend.

Chapter 6

Problem Solved

I'm sitting in this classroom and can't believe what I'm learning. Mom and Dad say they're proud of me. Sam says he's happy because he's learning how to swim and he feels better. Amy says it's the best summer ever.

That's right, Amy, my still-best friend and I are taking the two days of babysitter's and first aid training together. Amy is my partner, and this morning we practiced how to help somebody who is choking. And we will also get to have some fun in the sun. This is how it all worked out . . . .

The day after I watched Connie in the clinic, I went back to see her.

"Any questions from yesterday?" she asked me right off.

"What did you see when you looked in the baby's eyes?"

"I saw what we call a 'red reflex,' which means that the light goes through like it's supposed to. Plus, I looked at the size of the pupils and how they react to light."

"You could see all that in just a quick second? I can see why you had to study so much. Something else I wonder is if Mrs. Andrews was okay about feeding her baby when she left."

"Yes, she was. Crystal reassured her about the breastfeeding and Mrs. Andrews can call her anytime. Is that your journal?" Connie pointed to the notebook I was carrying.

"This is what I've been writing down about Sam's breathing after swimming. Mom and I thought you'd want to see it. He's doing really well." I gave her the book.

Connie checked my notes where I'd written when Sam had used the inhaler and how his breathing looked and sounded after swimming.

"This is excellent. What does Sam think about it?"

"He likes that I'm keeping a record. He's proud of himself, and he's really learning to swim now."

"That's good to hear. Do you have any new thoughts or questions about nurse practitioners?"

"I learned a *lot* from you. Like how important your job is. And what you need to know to do it all. But I still don't quite understand what the main difference is between a doctor and a nurse practitioner."

"That's a great question. Most of the time there's not a big difference in what a primary care doctor and I do. The doctor has more expertise in diagnosing and treating complicated problems. I handle the more usual problems, and I emphasize how to stay healthy. It's up to me to know what's normal or abnormal and when to contact a doctor. I spend more time teaching parents and children."

"Then that's what *I* want to do!"

But that didn't begin to tell her everything I wanted

to say. Last night I'd decided that Connie would want me to talk about what I'd learned. She had definitely helped me understand what she did for children and parents. For students, too. And about the world of nurse practitioners. So I pulled out my folder and showed her my notes.

"I'm going to look back at these when I get ready to decide on college. But I know right now that I want to be a nurse."

Connie looked over my notes. "These are really good descriptions of what we talked about, Nikki."

"What's best is that now I have a way to think about all of this."

"Really? Tell me what you mean."

"This is what I know for sure. First, you have to listen to what's inside of you and think about what it's telling you to do. Then, find people like you who will show you what they do for a career."

"That's like understanding your dream. Wow! You've accomplished a lot this summer." Connie reached out and shook my hand.

"There's more," I said. "When I told Amy what was in the babysitter's course, she said she wanted to take it with me. So we figured out that when her parents go to the beach she could stay overnight with me for two days while we go to class. Then my parents could drive us to the beach to join Amy's family."

"Did they agree?"

"Yes! Everybody liked our plan. And when I get back from the beach, I'm going to take a beginner's Spanish course for the last part of summer. Do you think when I'm old enough I could volunteer at your clinic?"

"When you're sixteen, we'd love to have you join us."

"And could I possibly come back to spend time with Michael? I like that his specialty is whole families. And with Crystal, too?"

Connie was nodding yes to everything. Even so, I felt like I was asking for a lot of favors.

"Of course you can do all of that. They both invited you, and they meant it."

"Thank you *so* much. Oh, and Sam wants me to ask you if he could spend time with a nurse practitioner when he's older. He can't wait to meet Michael."

"We'd love to have him join us in a few years. In the meantime, I'll be sure to have Michael say hello next time Sam comes for an appointment."

"I know you don't have much time now. But would you wait just a minute while I get Sam from the waiting room?"

"Sam is here?"

A minute later we were back, and Sam handed Connie the big pasted envelope he'd made last night. He stood on one foot and then the other, grinning.

Connie opened the envelope and pulled out the stiff paper with bright red, blue and yellow swirls around the edges.

"I painted the sides," Sam said. "See? The picture is of you and me. Nikki drew the people and I drew the bird and flowers." He pointed at each figure in the drawing and

the words "our hero" over Connie's figure. "We did the letter together and Nikki wrote it out."

"This is really special! I'm going to frame it for my office."

"I'll read it out loud to you," I said, and I did.

Dear Connie,

We both want to say thank you for always showing that you care. You go from one child to the next all day long without stopping, just like a hummingbird that flies from flower to flower.

You are so friendly that we are never afraid to go to the clinic. You teach us about growing up healthy and making good choices.

Thank you for taking the time to tell us all about what you do. Maybe someday we will be just like you!

Your Friends,

Nikki and Sam

The End

About the Author

Elaine Wick is an experienced pediatric nurse, educator and administrator with an advanced degree in maternal and child health nursing. She writes both fiction and non-fiction for children. She lives in Alexandria, Virginia with her husband and schnoodle puppy, Loki.

About the Illustrator

Michele Tremaine is an award-winning artist who writes and illustrates children's books.

Glossary

Advanced Practice Nursing (APN) — Nurses with master's degrees who have special practice requirements, such as a Pediatric Nurse Practitioner.

Anatomy — the study of the physical structure of animals, plants and other organisms; in people, the study of the body.

Assessment of health — Checking all aspects of a person's state of health.

Asthma — A condition of the respiratory (breathing) system that makes breathing hard due to swollen air passages that become narrower and full of mucus, making it more difficult for air to move in or out of the lungs.

Certified Nurse Midwife (CNM) — A specialist who is educated in the two disciplines of Nursing and Midwifery

Certified Registered Nurse Anesthetist (CRNA) — A specialist who is educated in the two disciplines of Nursing and Anesthesiology

Clinical Practice — The application of nursing skills.

Collaboration — Working together with one or more people to successfully achieve a goal.

Diagnosis — Identifying an illness or cause of a problem by using assessment, examinations and/or medical tests; deciding what is normal or abnormal.

Folliculitis — Infection of the hair follicles of the skin or scalp.

Immunizations — Also called vaccinations, the vaccines mobilize the body's immune system to prevent sickness caused by certain infectious diseases.

Inhaler — A small spray can-like tube containing medicine that is sprayed into the air passages to open them for easier breathing. Inhalers may have a spacer on one end that holds the medicine until it can be breathed in.

Integrity — Having and sticking to high moral principles; trustworthy.

Lymph Nodes — Small bodies of the lymph system that are found throughout the human body, and which help reduce infections.

Nebulizer — An air compressor machine that turns liquid medicine into a mist that is breathed in through a mask.

Nurse Practitioners — Advanced practice nurses, such as Pediatric Nurse Practitioners (PNP), Family Nurse Practitioners (FNP), Women's Health Nurse Practitioners (WHNP), and many others.

Pathophysiology — How the normal body and its organs change when a person gets sick or his health changes.

Peak Flow Meter — A hand-held device that measures how well air moves out of the lungs.

Pharmacology — The study of drugs/medicines, including their sources, make-up, how produced, how used and their effects.

Plan of Care/treatment — A plan that is made to return a child (or adult) to the best state of health. The plan may include good health practices, positive behaviors, medicines or referrals to specialists.

Pediatric Primary Care — Helping children to grow up healthy, and helping them with their illnesses, problems and needs (along with the parents).

Reflexes of newborn babies — A reflex is a response to a stimulus. Right after birth, certain responses in a baby show how well the baby is developing:

Rooting — baby's head turns and mouth opens when the cheek is stroked.

Moro (startle) — baby's arms spread and hands open when there is a sensation of loss of support.

Palmar grasp — when the baby's palm is stimulated with a finger, his hand grasps the adult's finger.

Stethoscope — A medical instrument used for listening to breathing, heartbeats, and other sounds made by the body.

Telehealth — Treatment by telephone or television using two-way links and other systems to discuss medical information.

For Further Reading

Books

R. N. Hope, *The Magic Stethoscope,* Fairfax, VA: College of Nursing and Health Science, George Mason University, 2002.
Written by nurses with lots of experience, this book of many stories shows the adventures that a career in nursing offers. The stories are taken from true experiences of the nurse authors, as seen through the eyes of two children.

Rae Simons and Viola Ruelke Gommer, *Nurse: Careers With Character,* Broomall, PA: Mason Crest Publishers, 2003.
This book about nurses and nursing talks mainly about the kind of personality needed for the job of nursing and how nurses touch the lives of others.

Cindy Klingel and Robert B. Noyed, *Nurses,* Minneapolis, MN: Compass Point Books, 2002.
Written for children up to third grade, this book explains some of the basics of nursing.

Barbara Sheen, *Asthma,* San Diego, CA: Lucent Books, The Gale Group, Inc., 2003.
This book gives an overview of asthma, the treatment, how to live with asthma and what the future holds.

Websites with Helpful Information

http://www.napnap.org

The National Association of Pediatric Nurse Practitioners provides information about this profession. Click on "Practice" then go to "What is a PNP?" for more information. Click on "Education" then go to "PNP Programs" to find out which universities offer this education.

http://www.nursesource.org

Nurses for a Healthier Tomorrow is a coalition of 42 nursing and health care organizations created to attract people to the profession of nursing. Explore this whole Website for lots of information about nursing as a career.

http://www.awhonn.org

This is a Website for an association that specializes in the care of women and newborn babies. Click on "Practice Resource Center" to read about careers in nursing that focus on women and infants.

http://www.nsna.org

The National Student Nurses' Association is an organization to help nurses who are still in school. Click on "Career Center" to see many tips on planning your career.

http://www.discovernursing.com

This Website by Johnson & Johnson will give you information on the "whys" and "hows" of choosing nursing as a profession, and you can read interviews of specific nurses.

http://www.redcross.org/services/hss/courses/community.html

At this Website, click on "Babysitter's Training" to learn about courses you can take for babysitting and first aid.

http://www.lungusa.org

The American Lung Association offers information about asthma and many other lung conditions.

To order additional copies of this book, contact:

National Association of Pediatric Nurse Practitioners (NAPNAP)
20 Brace Road, Suite 200
Cherry Hill, NJ 08034-2634
Telephone: 856/857-9700
www.napnap.org